This igloo book belongs to:

............................................

# Contents

igloobooks

Published in 2020
by Igloo Books Ltd
Cottage Farm
Sywell
NN6 0BJ

Copyright © 2020 Igloo Books Ltd
Igloo Books is an imprint of Bonnier Books UK

0720 002
ISBN: 978-1-83903-888-4

Written by Lucy Barnard
Illustrated by Cherie Zamazing

Designed by Kerri-Ann Hulme
Edited by Caroline Richards

Printed and manufactured in China

# 5 Minute Tales

# Pony Stories

igloobooks

# Little Willow

Willow woke one morning feeling very excited.
Today, she was going to explore the farm without her mum.

*After all, I'm big enough now,*

she thought and **crept** out of
the stable as quietly as possible.

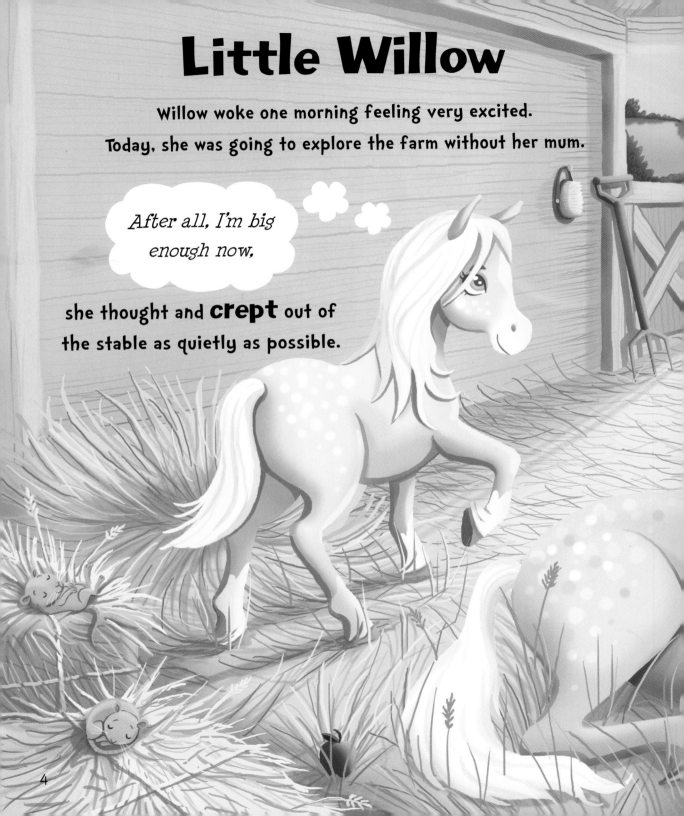

Willow trotted over to the henhouse.

*Martha and the other hens will be awake,*

she thought.

But the hens were having breakfast. They were so busy **squawking** at each other, they didn't even notice little Willow.

5

I'll say hello to Cedric and all the sheep!

said Willow, trotting over to them, full of excitement.

But the sheep were hurrying to the pasture. They all **bleated** and **baaed** at the same time. What a noise!

6

Willow felt quite dizzy.

I think I need to go somewhere a bit calmer. I know! I'll visit Bertie at the goat pen.

But the goats were having some sort of competition...

... and they hardly noticed Willow approaching.

As Willow got nearer, Bertie **flung** himself into a huge muddy puddle. Sticky mud flew through the air and landed **SPLAT!** all over Willow.

SPLODGE!

Yuck! That smells horrid!

she cried.

SQUELCH!

Just then, Daisy and the cows came round the corner on the way back from milking. They **barged** past and were so busy mooing, they didn't even see Willow...

... who was **swatted** by one long cow tail.

**Help!** cried Willow.

9

Just then, Willow's mum trotted around the corner.
Willow was so relieved to see her.

Willow said,

I wanted to explore
the farm on my own, but I
don't think anyone likes me.
They aren't friendly at all.

Everyone's busy in
the morning, that's all.
Come on, let's go round
the farm together.

said Mum, kindly,

So, Mum took Willow
to see everyone.

Hi, Willow!

clucked Martha
the hen.

Sorry about
earlier!

bleated Cedric
the sheep.

Didn't mean to
splash you,

apologised
Bertie.

You're so little,
we didn't see you.

said Daisy the cow,
mooing softly.

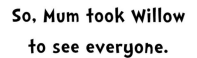

11

The farm is friendly, but you are too small to be by yourself. Promise me you won't go off on your own again?

**asked Mum.**

I promise. Not until I'm big!

**said Willow.**

12

Mum nuzzled Willow gently and said,

You'll always be Little Willow to me.

Everyone on the farm **bleated, mooed, baaed** and **cheeped** in agreement.

# Harry Saves the Day

Harry the carthorse had been at Greenacres Farm for as long as anyone could remember. He was gentle, kind and still **very** strong. But Harry worried that he might get too old to be of use.

Harry worried even more when two new ponies arrived at the farm. Tilly and Oscar were friendly, young and full of **energy**.

Their coats **gleamed**, and their eyes **shone**.

They could jump extra **high**...

... and run super **fast**.

15

All of Harry's other friends agreed, but Harry couldn't help feeling he was being replaced.

One spring morning, Tilly and Oscar seemed more giddy than usual. They were **prancing** around and **laughing** so much that they knocked into the hay cart.

It **rocked** to the side and then began to roll down the hill!

Tilly shouted out in alarm,

Oscar! We need to stop it!

I don't think we can!

yelled Oscar, beginning to panic.

The two ponies raced down the hill but weren't brave enough to step in front of the runaway cart.

Harry came out of his stable, wondering what all the fuss was about.

**Help!**

called Oscar.

Oh, no!

cried Harry,
in alarm.

The heavy cart was
**rumbling** straight
towards the sheep pen!

Harry **galloped** across
the paddock. He **thundered**
down the hill, past the cart.

Harry was so strong, he was able to slow
the cart down, and bring it to a stop.

"Oh, thank you!" said Freda in a wobbly voice.

"Harry's a hero!" cried Buttercup the cow.

"The bravest and strongest horse here!" agreed Tilly.

Now Harry knew he would always have a place at Greenacres Farm.

21

# Boastful Bonnie

The Big Show was days away and the ponies of Appletree Stables were all practising, except for the new arrival, Bonnie.

Look at my fabulous shiny coat and gleaming hooves. I'm sure to win a prize,

she boasted loudly.

Bonnie boasted all morning. She distracted Amber from jumping...

... interrupted Poppy's canter practice and disrupted Lily's trotting session.

Bonnie **bragged** about herself so much, the ponies thought that she must be good at everything.

23

When the ponies asked Bonnie to show off, they were very surprised!

Her trotting was **clumsy** and **awkward**...

... she **cantered** like an unsteady foal...

... and when she jumped, her flailing back legs knocked the poles off.

24

We thought you'd be graceful and stylish!

blurted out Amber.

Pony Show

Everyone will laugh at us at the show,

said Poppy.

I'm sorry. I don't know how to do it properly,

said Bonnie, feeling upset.

25

The other ponies decided to help. Amber worked patiently with Bonnie to show her the best way to **jump**...

... Lily gave Bonnie tips on how to **trot** beautifully...

... and Poppy showed her that **cantering** was all about rhythm and gracefulness.

The day of the Big Show arrived and Amber, Lily and Poppy all managed to win rosettes.

Bonnie felt nervous, and although she wasn't the best at cantering or jumping, she did get a rosette for Most Improved Pony in Show.

28

# Complaining Cara

Cara was forever complaining about one thing or another.

This hay is too chewy, my coat is too scratchy and this stable is too small!

said Cara.

She was always looking for attention, and **moaning** loudly to whoever would listen.

Henry, Jack and Bella were **fed up** with hearing Cara's complaints and stopped taking her seriously.

One day there really will be something wrong and **nobody** will believe you,

warned Henry, but Cara just carried on moaning.

Then, one sunny afternoon the ponies all had a race around the field. Jack won quite fairly, but as always, Cara complained.

Jack pushed me, the race wasn't fair,

she grumbled.

When no one agreed, Cara cantered away, **sulking.**

Cara ran to the far meadow, feeling very sorry for herself. She tossed her long mane in frustration and it got **tangled** in the fence.

**Ouch!**

she cried. She pulled but it was completely **stuck!**

The more Cara struggled, the more her
mane got caught. She called for help and
complained loudly but no one came.

Then it began to get dark, and Cara felt scared.
She wished someone would hear her.

The dark made Cara **jump** at every little sound and she was trying to stay brave, when there was a loud **rustling** noise. It was getting nearer and nearer until, suddenly, a shape **loomed** out of the shadows towards her.

Cara was so relieved when she realised it was **Bella!**

Thank you,

she sniffed, as Bella gently untangled her mane.

We thought you were making it up when you called for help, but I got worried when you didn't return,

explained Bella.

When the others found out Cara really
had been trapped, they felt awful.

Don't feel bad, I deserved it,
but I promise I won't complain
anymore. In fact, from now on I'll
be Cheerful Cara instead!

**she said with a grin.**

# Scared Stella

Stella wished that she could be like her brother, Spike.
He was brave and adventurous, while she was timid and scared.

While Spike was leaping over **scary** super-high jumps,
Stella was hiding behind the older ponies, Max and Rory.

39

Stella slowly plodded along behind.
But when they came to the stream,
Spike **skipped** over it and
**cantered** across the meadow.

We mustn't go far,

called Stella,
anxiously...

... but Spike just carried on.

Before long, Spike and Stella were a long way
from the paddock and it was beginning to rain.

Look, a wood!

cried Spike,
running off.

Come back!

neighed Stella.

She saw Spike disappear between the trees and felt afraid.

41

A **flash** of lightning lit up the woods and Stella could just see Spike **galloping** down the path.

Spike, come back!

she cried.

Just then, Stella heard a thunder **clap** and a loud shout for help. It was Spike.

Stella cantered along the path and found Spike stuck in a patch of **gloopy** mud.

I was going so fast, I **slipped** and I can't get out! You need to get help, Stella, it will be dark soon,

called Spike.

43

Stella took a deep breath. She was going to have
to be brave whether she wanted to or not.

Stella **trotted** back through the woods,
trying to remember the right way.

*I'll follow the
hoof prints,*

she thought.

Suddenly, lightning **flashed** making
her jump. Stella broke into a gallop and
didn't stop until she had reached home.

**Help!** Spike's stuck in the woods, we need to get to him now!

shouted Stella, as she cantered into the paddock.

Max and Rory **whinnied** and followed Stella as she galloped off, towards the distant woods.

It wasn't long before Spike was back on his feet, and limping home.

You showed real bravery, said Max.

Great work, Stella, agreed Rory.

Stella smiled shyly as the storm clouds parted and a beautiful rainbow filled the sky.

Thank you for being brave, you were amazing,

said Spike when they were safely home.

You're welcome,

said Stella, feeling rather proud of herself. She had faced her fears and was determined never to be Scared Stella again!